To Tamara and Maddie,
who are both highly-
intelligent terrestrial
primates – J.E.

For Lorcan (Constructican)
and Ruben (Grapenoid).
Brotherlings from very
different planets – M.O.

First published
2011 by Macmillan
Children's Books
a division of Macmillan
Publishers Limited
20 New Wharf Road,
London N1 9RR
Basingstoke and Oxford
Associated companies
throughout the world
www.panmacmillan.com

ISBN: 978-0-230-74815-6 (HB)
ISBN: 978-0-330-51741-6 (PB)

Text copyright © Jonathan Emmett 2011
Illustrations copyright © Mark Oliver 2011
Moral rights asserted.
You can find out more about Jonathan Emmett's
books at www.scribblestreet.co.uk

The inclusion of author website addresses in this
book does not constitute an endorsement by or
association with Macmillan Publishers of such sites
or the content, products, advertising or other materials
presented on such sites.

1 3 5 7 9 8 6 4 2

A CIP catalogue record for this book
is available from the British Library.

Printed in Belgium by Proost

ALIENS
AN OWNER'S GUIDE

woof!

(JONATHAN EMMETT)

MARK OLIVER

MACMILLAN CHILDREN'S BOOKS

YOUR FIRST ALIEN

Aliens can make great pets, they're playful and they're clever.

Treat one with respect and it will be your friend forever.

But they can be demanding and quite difficult to feed.

So make sure that you can give them all the time and care they need.

KEY

1 Plunge-Footed Quirk
2 Blistering Guff
3 Lesser-Frazzled Worrit
4 Gassy Grib
5 Unidentified Exotic Species
6 Dribbling Crimps
7 Ogling Periscoptrix
8 Riddled Snoop
9 Bandy-Legged Wumph
10 Chattering Nabster
11 Hyronomous Bish
12 Phantabulous Squib
13 Bell-Bottomed Gawp
14 Blue-Oodled Bork (B.O.B.)
15 Tufted Clench
16 Ravenous Giger
17 Bog-Eyed Munster
18 Copious Thrang

CHOOSING THE RIGHT EGG

It's best to buy your alien before its egg has hatched.

Check the shell is in one piece and is not scuffed or scratched.

Avoid an egg that snarls or shrieks or mutters monstrous threats.

You can be sure that angry eggs will not make ideal pets.

LOOKING AFTER YOUR EGG

- ☑ Handle your egg carefully.
- ☒ Don't drop or let it fall.
- ☒ Don't tap or shake or spin it.
- ☒ Don't treat it as a ball.

When you've got it home,
your egg will need a cosy nest.
Expensive duvets are ideal,
a shredded one is best!

WHEN YOUR EGG HATCHES

Your alien may hatch at any time of day or night,

so stay beside it constantly to check that it's all right.

First the egg will start to shudder, then the shell will start to crack.

Then the egg will explode outwards, so remember . . .

SAYING HELLO

A newborn baby alien has
a strong unpleasant smell,
so have a clothes peg handy,
and a sick bucket as well.

Its skin is thickly coated in
a gooey, greenish scum.
But it's ESSENTIAL that you hug it,
so it thinks you are its mum.

SMELL-O-METER

FLOWERS SOCKS FISH PANTS

FEEDING AND DIET

Your alien will be hungry and will need something to eat.

But you shouldn't feed it Earth food such as vegetables or meat.

Any glass or plastic makes a healthy alien meal,

but metal is their favourite, especially stainless steel!

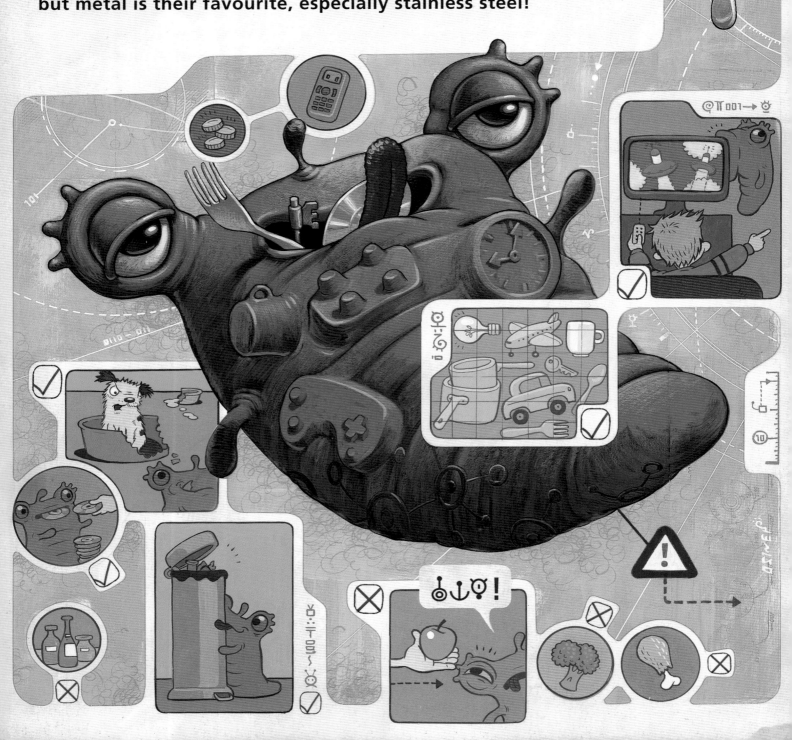

TOILET TRAINING

Alien pee is acid and will eat right through your floor.

And alien poop is unlike any poop you've seen before!

You won't believe just how much poop one alien can produce.

So it's VITAL that your alien is trained in toilet use.

COPING WITH COCOONS

A few days after hatching, often in the afternoon, your alien will start to spin a colourful cocoon.

This thick protective casing will keep it nice and warm, while its body is rebuilt into . . .

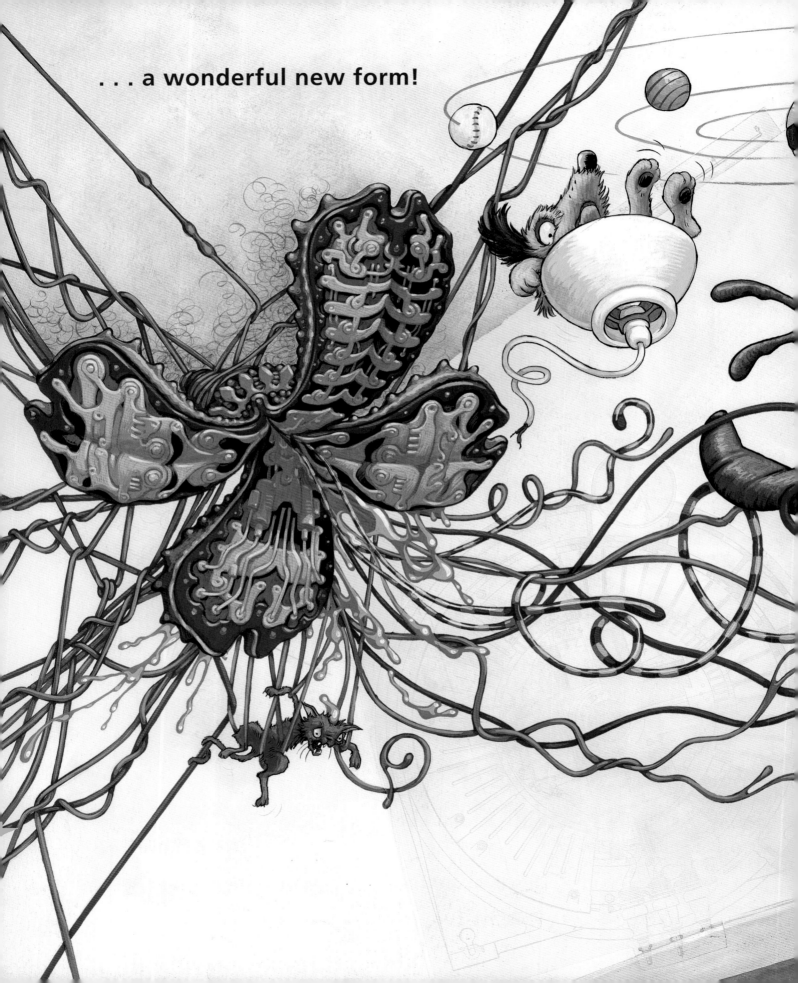

. . . a wonderful new form!

LET'S PLAY!

Aliens are playful, inquisitive and smart.

They're very good at making things and taking things apart.

Encourage them to play with you and let them share your toys.

You'll find it's an experience that everyone enjoys.

MIXING WITH OTHER ALIENS

Aliens would usually be found in family groups.

They talk to one another using whistles, clicks and whoops.

But as your pet grows older, and gets smarter, it will try to call to other aliens, who will usually reply.

SAYING GOODBYE

As the owner of an alien you should always keep in mind,

that one day your pet creature will leave this world behind.

Try not to be too sad, it is natural – and who knows,

if you're very, very lucky . . . ----▶

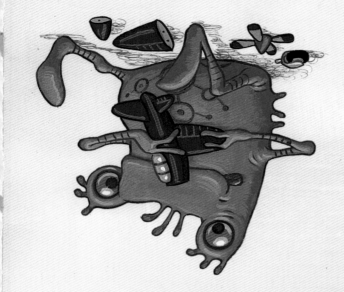